dangerous mop searching for prey

lurking industrial-size paper towel roll

Amelia's School Survival Guide

by Marissa Moss
(and fearless guide Amelia!)

Now if I can just get out of this janitor's closet!

Simon & Schuster
Books for Young Readers
New York   London
Toronto   Sydney

ruler (can be used as splint if necessary) ↑

This guide is dedicated
to Asa,
an expert on school already!

pencil box
(or emergency
writing rations)

notebook
(or crisis
management
papers)

SIMON & SCHUSTER BOOKS FOR YOUNG READERS
An imprint of Simon & Schuster
Children's Publishing Division
1230 Avenue of the Americas, New York, New York 10020
Copyright © 2002 by Marissa Moss

First SIMON & SCHUSTER BOOKS FOR YOUNG READERS
edition, 2006

SIMON & SCHUSTER BOOKS FOR YOUNG READERS
IS A TRADEMARK OF SIMON & SCHUSTER, INC.

Amelia ® and the notebook design are
registered trademarks of Marissa Moss.

Book design by Amelia
(with help from Jessica Sonkin)

The text for this book is hand-lettered.

Manufactured in China
2 4 6 8 10 9 7 5 3 1

CIP data is available from the Library of
Congress.
ISBN-13: 978-1-4169-0915-6
ISBN-10: 1-4169-0915-X

compass
(not the kind that
helps out in the
wilderness, but useful
for untamed math
problems)

glue stick
(or critical adhesive
support)

protractor
(for covering all the
angles)

scissors
(to cut to the
chase)

School is about to start and NO WAY do I want to make the same mistakes that I made last year. So I'm writing this guide to be sure I do things RIGHT.

I'll start with **10** school year resolutions.

1. This year I will NOT call my teacher "Mom" by mistake.

Mom, uh...
I mean, Ms. Busby?

cheeks bright red →

stomach suddenly queasy →

floor I want to sink into
↓

2. I solemnly swear that I will always have at least _two_ sharpened pencils with me.

I write better, sharper ideas with a nice pencil tip. Blunt tips make my ideas clunky.

3. I hereby vow to try to get to school early so that I can see my friends before class starts.

Carly

Leah

It will put me in a good mood if I can begin my day talking with Carly and Leah.

4. I promise, cross my heart, to return all my library books on time, so I'll always get to check out new ones.

moldy dark corner

What's _this_ book doing here? I checked it out _years_ ago. I don't want to know what the overdue fine is!

BOO!

ghost book that will haunt you if you don't let its pages rest in peace - in the library!

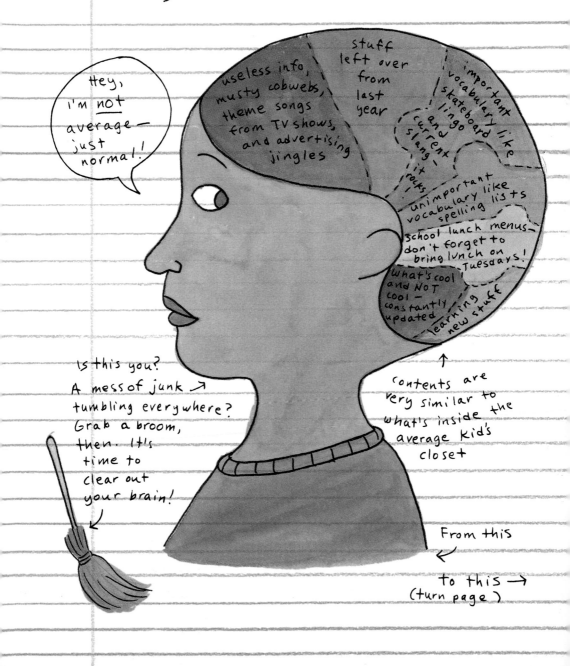

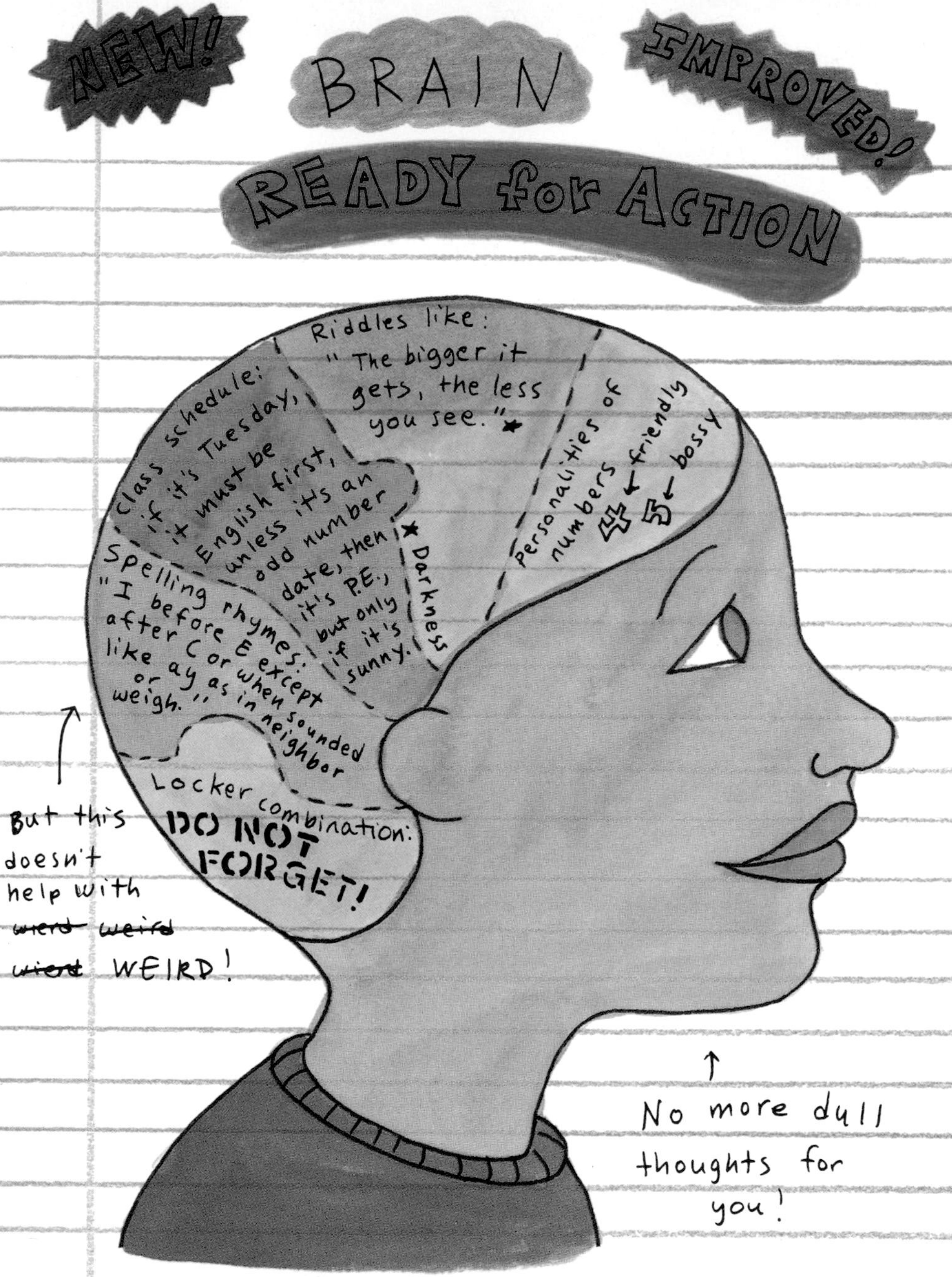

NEW!
BRAIN
IMPROVED!
READY for ACTION
Riddles like: "The bigger it gets, the less you see."*
Class schedule: if it's Tuesday, it must be English first, unless it's an odd number date, then it's P.E., but only if it's sunny.
*Darkness
Personalities of numbers
4 ← friendly
5 ← bossy
Spelling rhymes: "I before E except after C or when sounded like ay as in neighbor or weigh."
Locker combination: DO NOT FORGET!
But this doesn't help with ~~wierd~~ ~~weird~~ ~~wiord~~ WEIRD!
No more dull thoughts for you!

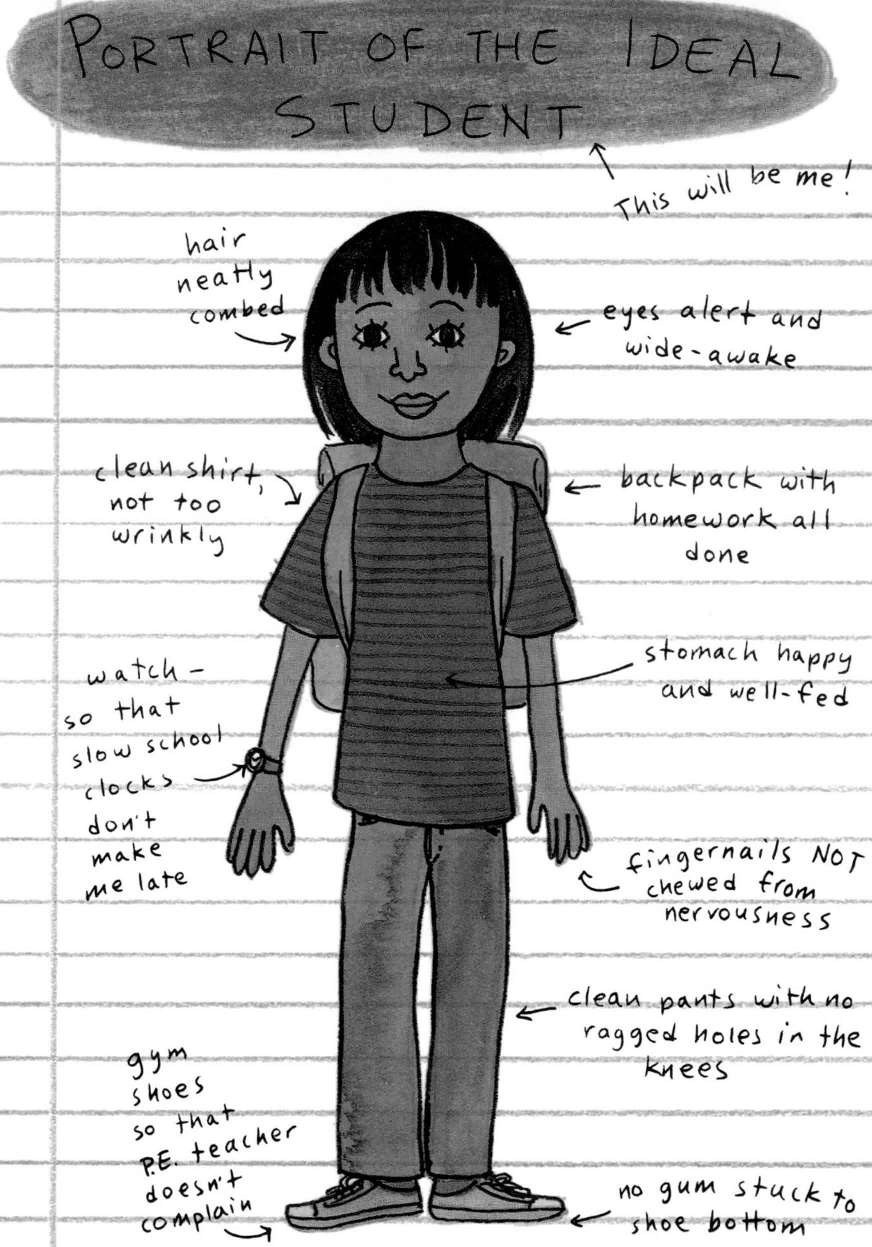
PORTRAIT OF THE IDEAL STUDENT
This will be me!
hair neatly combed
eyes alert and wide-awake
clean shirt, not too wrinkly
backpack with homework all done
stomach happy and well-fed
watch - so that slow school clocks don't make me late
fingernails NOT chewed from nervousness
clean pants with no ragged holes in the knees
gym shoes so that P.E. teacher doesn't complain
no gum stuck to shoe bottom

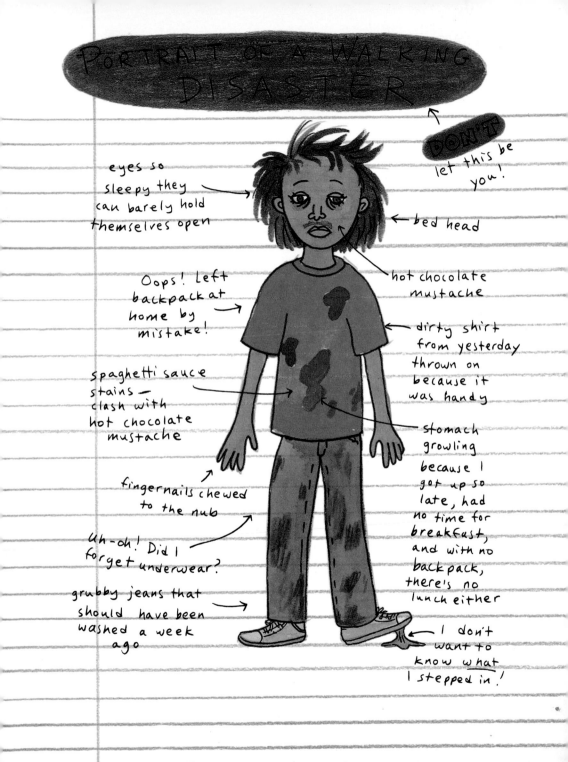

NOT ABC'S

OR HOW TO HANDLE EMERGENCIES...

Band-Aid for paper cuts

To resuscitate your brain after lethal lectures have bored it to death, take DEEP breaths and think of knock-knock jokes. Slowly but surely, your brain will revive.

I can't stop yawning!

hot water bottle for cramped hands tired of taking notes

To eat cafeteria food without gagging, practice stomach control. Eat only as much as is absolutely necessary and plug your nose if it's REALLY bad. (Don't look, either.)

Both these cures will work at home, too — use in case of bad home cooking or predictable parental lecture.

BUT S.O.S!

... NOT INVOLVING LOSS OF BLOOD

If someone steals your lunch and you know who the thief is, say something to make them really regret that they ate it.

crutches for foot injured by falling backpack

ice pack for head-ache caused by massive homework

Oh, I hope you didn't eat my lunch by mistake. I have a heart condition, and my mom hides my medicine in my dessert. It doesn't make the food taste bad.

But it could give you a heart attack.

Suddenly, I feel VERY sick!

If someone is mean to you and calls you names, think of the strangest word you can and call them that.

It can be impossible to avoid bullies, but it's NOT impossible to stand up for yourself!

You're a klorgag-fiserket!

no swear-words so you don't get in trouble

Huh?

They'll spend days trying to figure out what it is you called them.

My gorilla's bigger than yours!

Amelia's Guide

The Monotone Mumbler

This teacher can be recognized chiefly by his **voice**. He says everything in exactly the same tone, as if he were reading the phone book.

eyes barely even blink →

gray clothes to match gray voice →

mouth never opens wider than this

hands never gesture— that would be too expressive

drab shoes with no personality to go with drab everything else

DANGER: You might fall asleep in class! To keep your eyes open, draw a chart of how you wish his voice would rise and fall.

Helpful Hint: wear tight underwear — the pain will keep you awake!

THE rain in Spain falls mainly ON the plain.

to Teachers

The Homework Heaper

This teacher piles on so much homework, you don't have time for ANYTHING else. DON'T groan that it's too much or she might give you more. ("I'll show you too much!") DO try bargaining with her.

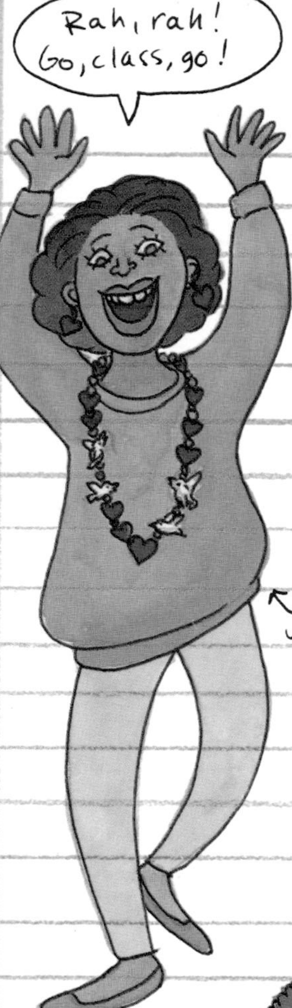

The Chatty Cheerleader

This teacher has a <u>lot</u> of enthusiasm for everything—even fire drills. Show team spirit and she'll be happy. Make up your own cheers and she'll be ecstatic!

↖ wears bright colors and theme jewelry (like spiders for Halloween and cranberry necklaces for Thanksgiving)

Helpful Hint: Get into the spirit and join the team—it'll be more fun!

The Gruff Grump

This teacher has been working too hard for too long. Don't get on his bad side. (I know, you're asking what other side *is* there?) And try not to be grumpy yourself or things will get even worse.

Helpful Hint:
Try whatever you can to cheer him up. He might lose some of his gruffness. (But I don't promise it.)

The Doormat Teacher

This teacher is usually (but not always) a substitute. You can tell a Doormat by her inability to control kids. Having students run the class can be fun for a day or two, but gets BOOOOOOORING after a while.

DANGER: Doormats can go from being walked all over to being <u>run</u> all over — watch out for stampedes!

Helpful Hint: Protect this delicate endangered species by telling the other students to listen to her — show her your respect.

The Perfect Teacher

This is not a mythological creature, but a rare breed indeed. You'll be lucky to have 1 specimen from this genus in all the years you go to school. But one is all you need, because this teacher is so exciting you'll never forget her. You'll recognize her by her ability to open up your brain to completely new things.

head full of terrific ideas

usually holding something interesting

even more likely to have a book in her hand — books are one of her favorite things

It's hard not to love this teacher— so go ahead!

Helpful Hint: You may not recognize this species at first — they can be camouflaged, but with time their talents shine!

She'll have you doing stuff you never thought you could do — and that's a great lesson in itself!

INTERPRETING

Talking to teachers can be like talking to another species!

(Meow!)

(Arf!)

(BAAA!)

(Mooo)

(eeeek)

(ssss)

(ROAR!)

"This won't count for a grade." = Oh, yes it does!

"This will take a little extra work." = Better spend the whole weekend on it!

"Extra credit" = You get a second chance — don't blow it!

"Standardized test" = long, boring test where the first question is "Do you have the right kind of pencil to take the test in the first place?"

"Work independently at home." = If your project doesn't have lumps of glue and sloppy corners, I'll know a grown-up did it.

TEACHER TALK

"I'm disappointed with how you did this." = You have to do it over.

Do you plant stink bombs in class?

"Is that clear? Any questions?" = Ask now or forever hold your peace.

"Class, I have a special surprise today!" = Today we're seeing a filmstrip on mushroom spores.

PSST!

Do you pass notes often?

"I want to see your work on these math problems." = No chicken-scratches allowed. You'd better make those numbers look like numbers!

Wasn't the War of 1812 in 1812?

"Teachers don't have favorites." = If I have a favorite, I'm definitely not telling you!

Do you point out your teacher's mistakes?

If you answered yes to any of these, chances are good that you're NOT a teacher's pet! →

PURRRR

What Kind of

1. What kind of mood do you need to be in to do homework?

Do you cover your books with: ↓

A. calm and collected	B. happy, listening to music	C. utter desperation
Books here, paper there, pens over there — all set!	I write better to the beat.	AWK! This is all due TOMORROW!

↑ wallpaper?

2. What do you do when the teacher asks for someone to go first for an oral report?

↑ paper bags?

A. Raise your hand so you can get it over with.	B. Look at the person next to you as a likely candidate.	C. Suddenly need to go to the bathroom.
Might as well...	You go, you go, you go...	It's definitely time to go!

← fly paper?

Student Are You?

3. What do you do when you forget your homework?

A. Admit that you forgot it	B. Give an inventive excuse	C. Tell your mom you're too sick to go to school

- "I'm sorry!"
- "I was abducted by aliens and only returned in time to make it to school!"
- "I have a horrible headache and I'm seeing spots!"

Is your backpack:

↓

light and easy to carry? (You've got to be dreaming! What school do you go to?)

4. What do you do when you know the answer to a question?

A. Raise your hand and wait to be called on	B. Lean forward and wave your hand wildly	C. Blurt out the answer, you're so excited to know it

eager-eyed and polite →

- "Oh, oh, oh! I know! I know! Pick me!"
- "It's Godzilla!"

↑ heavier than you?

"It's a tough job, but someone's got to do it."

on rollers and pulled by a weight-lifter, it's so hard to budge

5. For extra credit, you always choose projects that are...

The school supply you use most is

↓

an eraser

A. encyclopedic	B. artistic	C. edible

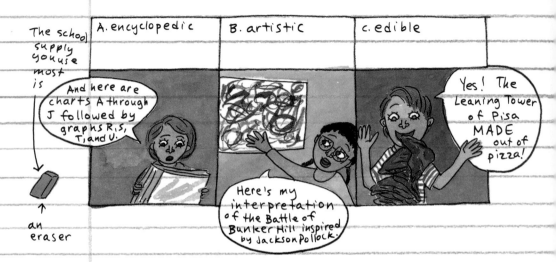

And here are charts A through J followed by graphs R, S, T, and U.

Here's my interpretation of the Battle of Bunker Hill inspired by Jackson Pollock.

Yes! The Leaning Tower of Pisa MADE out of pizza!

6. If you're running late for school, you skip...

a calculator

↑

A. breakfast	B. brushing your hair	C. first period

No time — I'll eat at recess!

Running will mess it up anyway — might as well go for the natural look.

I'm right on time for my second class!

a hole punch

↑

Whee! I love making confetti! →

your favorite non-school supply is: →

dried noodles for art projects

felt — you can use it a zillion ways

dry ice — cool for creepy effects!

7. How do you treat substitute teachers?

A. You help them with the class routine.	B. You help them with the class routine.	C. You help them with the class routine.
"We usually have 15 minutes of silent reading now."	"We're doing special research on recess now, so we're supposed to have an extra hour outside."	"I have a private tutoring session now — I'll see you tomorrow." "Bye!"

If you answered mostly A's:

You're a perfect student. Teachers love you. You may even be a teacher's pet.

If you answered mostly B's:

If your teacher has a sense of humor, you get along fine. If your teacher is a grump — watch out! And if your mom sits in on your class one day, you're in trouble!

If you answered mostly C's:

Sorry, you're not the teacher's pet. Try participating more. You might have more fun if you were more "there" there.

NOTE-TAKING

DO keep your notes in the same predictable place, so you'll always know where to find them.

DO write notes that are useful.

DO bother to read your notes again before the test — otherwise why take them?

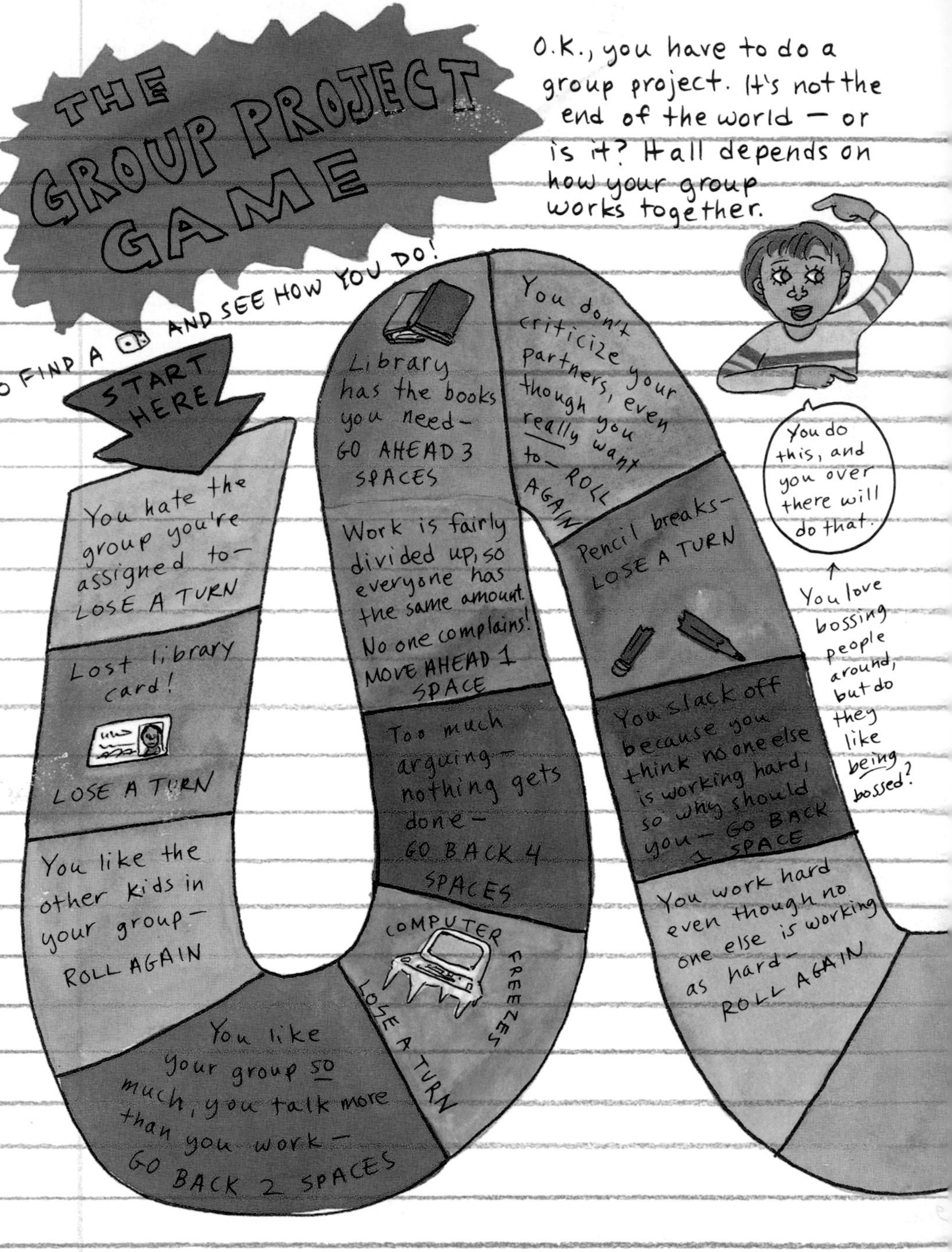

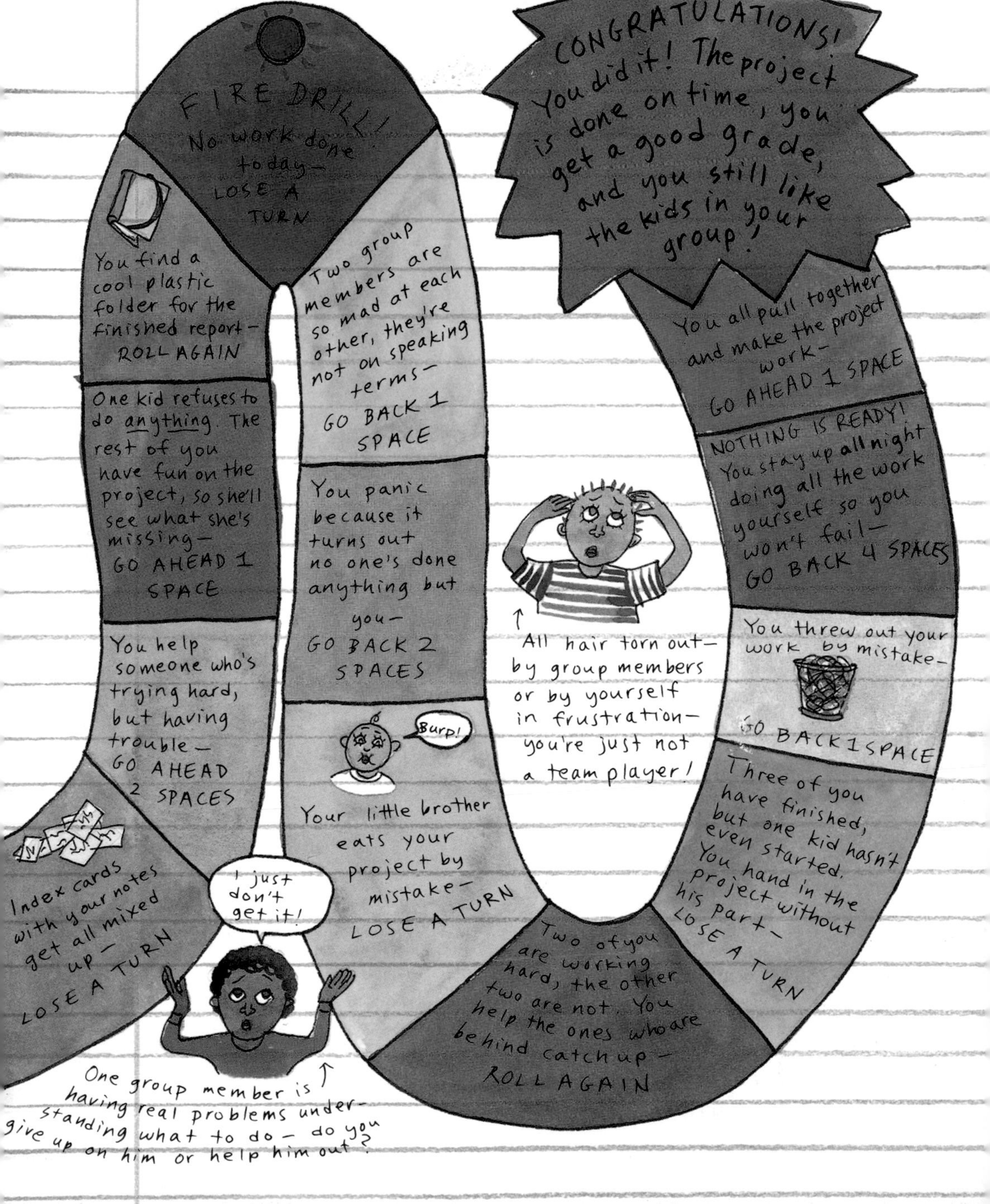
Index cards with your notes get all mixed up— LOSE A TURN
You help someone who's trying hard, but having trouble— GO AHEAD 2 SPACES
One kid refuses to do anything. The rest of you have fun on the project, so she'll see what she's missing— GO AHEAD 1 SPACE
You find a cool plastic folder for the finished report— ROLL AGAIN
FIRE DRILL! No work done today— LOSE A TURN
Two group members are so mad at each other, they're not on speaking terms— GO BACK 1 SPACE
You panic because it turns out no one's done anything but you— GO BACK 2 SPACES
Burp!
Your little brother eats your project by mistake— LOSE A TURN
I just don't get it!
One group member is having real problems under-standing what to do— do you give up on him or help him out?
Two of you are working hard, the other two are not. You help the ones who are behind catch up— ROLL AGAIN
Three of you have finished, but one kid hasn't even started. You hand in the project without his part— LOSE A TURN
You threw out your work by mistake— GO BACK 1 SPACE
NOTHING IS READY! You stay up all night doing all the work yourself so you won't fail— GO BACK 4 SPACES
You all pull together and make the project work— GO AHEAD 1 SPACE
CONGRATULATIONS! You did it! The project is done on time, you get a good grade, and you still like the kids in your group!
All hair torn out— by group members or by yourself in frustration— you're just not a team player!

Nimble

Numbers can be tricky to deal with — they're wily and elusive. But here are some hints to help you tame these capricious beasts. You can't treat all numbers alike (or you do so at your own peril). It's essential to understand each number's nature, so you can handle it right.

Grrrr!

Fives may look jolly — until they bare their teeth! Don't be fooled! They're often snappish and bite, especially when by themselves. In groups, they're easier to approach.

I wuv you!

Twos look a lot like fives upside-down and backwards, but they're completely different in temperament. Known for their sweet, cuddly nature, twos make wonderful pets.

Fours are the fairest of numbers. They make terrific judges and can intervene if there's a fight between other numbers.

Well, it can be this way...

...or I see how it can be that way.

Think of all the things there are seven of — seven seas...

Sevens love to have fun. They think they're lucky — and they're right! The more sevens you have, the better!

...seven days of the week, seven wonders of the world...

Numbers

Eights are the joke-tellers of the number family. It's always great to have an eight around!

> Did you hear why six is afraid of seven?

> Because seven eight nine!

> And what did the zero say to the eight?

> "Nice belt you've got!"

> Aren't you ecstatic to have me around?

Ones are complete snobs. They think they're first in everything. Flattery goes a long way with them. Otherwise, watch out! Their vanity is easily offended.

> YAWN! Is it a school day today?

Nines are a bit slow, as if they're always half-asleep. But with some prodding, you can get them to work for you.

> pleeeeze don't hurt me! pleeeze!

Sixes are worrywarts and fearful of everything. Don't make sudden moves or they'll faint in terror. If you're gentle, you can keep a six calm and under control. If you're not, it can be a disaster!

> Let's go bungee jumping! Wheeee!

Threes are unpredictable. Sometimes they behave well. Other times they're absolutely wild. You can <u>never</u> control them, but you won't be bored with them, either.

5. When you finish a test, you...

A. chant a charm to ensure success.	B. feel sick because you've chewed your pencil down to the stub.	C. check your answers to make sure you haven't missed anything.

6. When you get your test back, you...

A. give out bubble gum cigars, you're so proud and happy.	B. wait until you can't stand it anymore, then look at your grade.	C. look calm on the outside, but on the inside, you're cheering.

gold star
for
good work

happy
face for
a job
well done

If you answered mostly A's:
you rely on luck too much — start
using your brain! This is school, not a
lottery!

If you answered mostly B's:
you're not relying on anything — no wonder you're
so worried. Start studying and you'll feel a LOT better!

If you answered mostly C's:
you're a test-taking expert — congratulations!
(And can you help me study for my next test,
please?)

What I'd like to
see on tests

ALIEN
GOOD JOB FOR AN EARTHLING
EXTRA
CREDIT

COUPON
GOOD   FOR 1
SLICE OF PIZZA

GOOD WORK
SEAL OF APPROVAL

seal of approval

HISTORY

DON'T make a hash out of names and dates. History can be your friend! Add these handy-dandy ingredients to any history report and you'll earn extra points — money back guaranteed!*

For extra spice and sizzle include at least one famous name and what that person might have said about whatever it is you're writing.

for example

As Columbus would have seen it, there was no point in building the Great Wall of China. "Why cross on land when you can go by boat?"

or

George Washington felt lucky he wasn't in London during the Great Plague. "Ooh, yuck, gross — I hate nasty diseases like that! Wooden teeth are bad enough."

* That is, I guarantee you'll want your money back, but too bad, it'll be too late for that! Now isn't that a lesson worth learning in itself?

HELPER

To add meat to your report, don't forget to put in details about daily life. Kings and queens are important, but so are peasants and servants.

I didn't say "Let them eat cake." I said this wig is killing me!

And with all the tea dumped into Boston Harbor, what were we supposed to drink?

servant girl

↑Marie Antoinette

That's when I invented lemonade—yum!

The secret ingredient for your report can be a drawing, a map, a chart—make it something fun!

postage stamp from Pony Express (Hey! Were bicycles invented back then?)

actual replica of ticket for the Titanic

Admit One (No Icebergs Allowed.)

HOW TO CONQUER

I feel dizzy.

Don't look down!

Do you have a taste for adventure? Do you thirst for challenges? Do you hunger for wide-open spaces? Maybe you should have a good meal! OR you could try facing the

SAVAGE ORAL REPORT!

ORALUS REPORTUS, the most feared of school monsters — can cause sweaty palms and queasy stomachs even at great distances.

ORAL REPORTS

To face this beast, you need a cool head, calmness in the face of adversity, and great courage.

As it fixes its evil eyes on you and you feel its hot breath on your face, don't tremble or let your voice quaver. It will smell your fear and grow bolder. The essential thing is to speak LOUDLY, CLEARLY, and SLOWLY (well, not _too_ slow). Let your voice do the work. If you're prepared (and you'd better be!), your voice will carry you through.

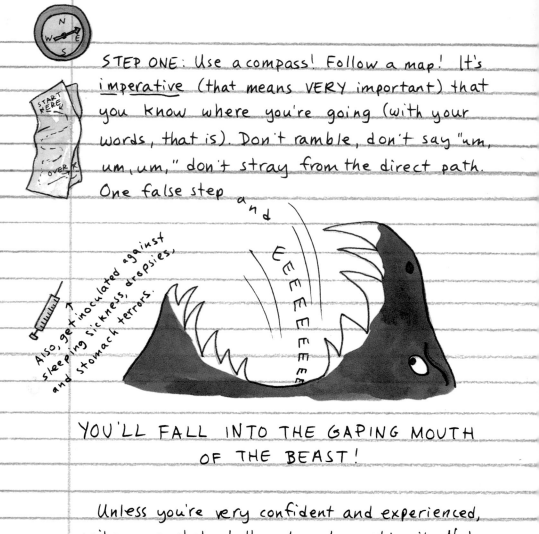

STEP ONE: Use a compass! Follow a map! It's imperative (that means VERY important) that you know where you're going (with your words, that is). Don't ramble, don't say "um, um, um," don't stray from the direct path. One false step and

EEEEEEEEEEEE

START HERE →

← OVER

Also, get inoculated against sleeping sickness, dropsies, and stomach terrors.

YOU'LL FALL INTO THE GAPING MOUTH OF THE BEAST!

Unless you're very confident and experienced, write your whole talk out and practice it. Notes are not enough. But read your report like you're talking to a friend. Otherwise, it'll be BOOORING. And bored beasts can be NASTY!

STEP TWO: Know your stuff! Know what you're talking about, and you can actually relax and have fun. The monster may still be threatening, its teeth may still be sharp, but facing your fears can be

EXHILARATING!

Especially when you feel up to the task, trained, and ready to go!

wheee! It's a snap!

Wow! Oral reports are more fun than bungee jumping!

You're not terrified of me?

SPICE UP

YOUR BOOK REPORT

← Bare-bones book report is like a stick figure.

Adding details gives more personality. →

Recipe for sweet success:

1. Add details! Don't just say you like a character, say you like his twinkly eyes or her hopscotch skills — give a reason why.

2. Explain how the book made you feel (bored, sad, happy, nervous, hungry — maybe it's a cookbook) and what parts made you feel that way most.

3. Is there something in the book you would change? The ending? A character? The useful information at the back of the book?

4. Pretend you're reviewing the book for other kids. Who do you think should read it? Why?

sour lemon ↓

↑ sour grapes

↑ sweet and sour

Read it because I SAID SO!

↖ This approach won't work.

Then he heard a knock. Then he opened the door. Then he saw it. Then he screamed. Then it ate him.

...then I fell asleep.

Recipe for extra-spicy reports:
1. Don't say "then" and "then" and "then" unless you want to put your reader to sleep. Try writing your report as if it were an argument between two people or as if it were a news story on something that really happened.

Reporting live from Alabama, where a blind-deaf girl has shown the world she can break down the walls between herself and others.

She's Helen Keller!

2. Try making a comic strip book report for something really different.

Yessir, I'm having soooo much fun painting!

Wow, Tom, can I try, please?

Well, dunno.

Maybe...

Please, let me try! Just a little! Please, please, please, Please, PLEASE!

Oh, go ahead!

Add as many sound effects as you can.

POW!

PUFF!

ZAP!

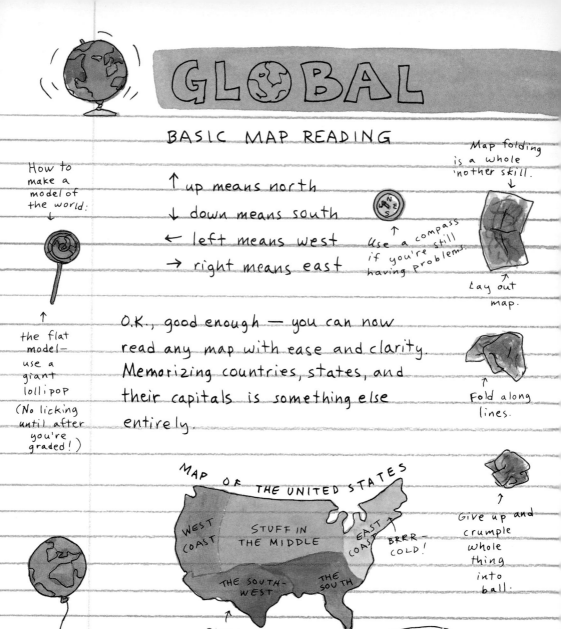

UNDERSTANDING

World Factoids
↓

"Howdy!"

↑
Penguins live in Antarctica, not the Arctic.

↑
A roll is a continental breakfast.

BASIC GEOGRAPHY
A continent is a big land mass (but a continental breakfast is a very small breakfast).

<u>A</u> country can be big or little.
<u>The</u> country is where there are farms.

More World Factoids
↓

Earth is 3/4 water— way more ocean than land!

"Wish you were here!"

"MOOO!"

"I'm from the country, but I live in the country of Switzerland."

"That's good news if you're a fish!"

↑
Polar bears live in the Arctic, not Antarctica.

There, that's as basic as you can get. If you want to know where Surinam is or which country is the biggest, better get yourself an atlas, not a survival guide.

But there are more insects than any other creatures.
↓

"So there, fishies!"

Two-hump camels come from Asia.
→

"I'm better!"

"No, I am!"

"One-hump camels come from Africa."

Creativity Crunch

Don't take a bite — it's not that kind of crunch!

No, I'm not talking about a candy bar, but about that tight feeling your head gets when your teacher expects you to be creative ON DEMAND. Teachers think assignments like "write a poem or a story" are easy. Ha! It's not like you just switch on a button and become instantly full of great ideas.

← the eater

the sensitive soul

I'll think of something AFTER this snack.

You can't command genius — you simply wait for it to strike.

I must wait for the muse to visit me.

the organizer

I'll do my math homework first. At least that has a clear beginning and end.

Just start writing — ANYTHING! Turn off your brain and let your pen go, like a Ouija board. Some of what you write may be pretty silly, but some of it could be the best you've ever written!

Skip the first page — go right to the middle or end. Write your paper backward!

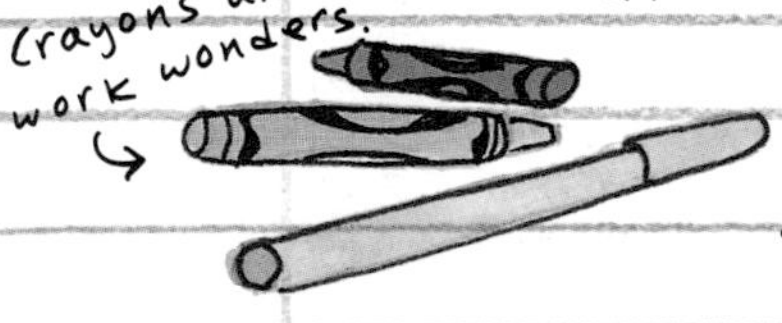

Start with a drawing. Sometimes a picture can give you ideas!

SENSATIONAL

No volcanoes or plants allowed! ↓

🚫

Why settle for the ordinary when you can have the EXTRAordinary? Here are some science fair projects I'd like to see!

🚫

MAKE A ROBOT

Think these projects aren't realistic? How about just doing part of them? ↓

Then train it to do all your homework AND clean your room!

SHOVING CLOTHES UNDER THE BED IS NOT PROPER CLEANING. I WILL SHOW YOU HOW IT SHOULD BE DONE.

Feel the muscle here! ↑

↑ not a whole robot, but a robotic arm

TRAIN YOUR HAMSTER

With careful scientific methods, teach your pet to perform amazing tricks and demonstrate a profound understanding of human speech. ↓

START

So what you're saying is that you want me to run through the maze and find the peanut? All that work for just a goober? Are you nuts?

↑ or simpler yet, a circuit— connect the wires and light the bulb!

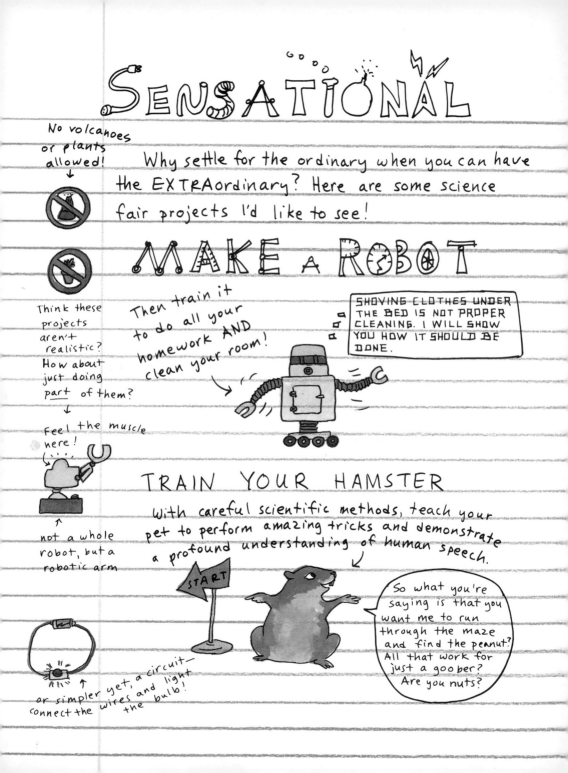

TO BRING LUNCH

← paper   or plastic →

If you pack a lunch, these guidelines will ensure a safe, pleasant eating experience. You're already a step ahead, since at least you know you won't get food poisoning from the cafeteria.

Look at the bench BEFORE you sit down.

Don't sit next to anyone who sticks straws up his nose.

Don't trade food unless you know what you're getting.

OR NOT TO  BRING LUNCH

edible or inedible?

If you're a real daredevil and willing to risk your stomach with cafeteria food, you'd better observe the following rules:

Oops!

Keep an extra shirt in your backpack so if the sloppy joe is <u>really</u> sloppy, you don't have to wear sauce all day.

← Extra pants and shoes could be handy, too.

No matter how hungry you are, don't eat anything you can't identify.

Mold is NOT a good sign. Suspicious lumps are to be avoided and if it's moving, don't put it on your fork!

BALL IN GYM:
DON'T get too close to someone doing jumping jacks.
WHAP!
PINA
DON'T chew gum while running.
Puff, puff- GLORP! Uh,oh!
gum bulge
Be sure to write your locker combination in a safe place.
Yikes! The number wore off of the bottom of my foot! But I never wash there — what happened?
Eeee! I'm falling!
NEVER say the reason you missed the volleyball is because you didn't want to chip a fingernail.
What? And ruin my perfect nails?

HOW DO YOU

1. The best conditions for you to do homework are:

A. at a neat, organized desk.	B. while eating a snack and watching TV.	C. while on safari in Africa.

You like your homework to be:

portable ↓

↑ easy-carry case — no big, heavy textbook

2. You like to do homework...

A. as soon as you get home from school.	B. after you've had a chance to relax for a while.	C. right before it's due.

edible ↓

← Spanish mission made of brownies — yum!

which of the following counts as homework?

cleaning toilets

folding laundry →

gluing macaroni on cardboard

5. Your favorite kind of homework is...

A. long reports that you can put in a fancy folder.	B. projects.	c. personal research in uncharted territory.
Now that looks professional!	Ta-da! The Alamo made of Jell-O!	At last I can discover how many licks it takes to finish a giant lollipop!

If you answered mostly A's:
   Homework is no problem for you — you're an expert
   and can juggle 3 projects at a time.

If you answered mostly B's:
   You're creative in doing your homework —
   especially in thinking of ways NOT to do it!

If you answered mostly C's:
   Homework and you are not always compatible,
   but you have a great sense of adventure.

FAMOUS PROJECTS

IN THE ANNALS OF HOMEWORK HISTORY

Lindsay's diorama of her backyard for her wilderness project

Clive's dust-bunny exhibit for the science fair

Stella's model of the Empire State Building made out of Life Savers (sucked on, of course)

Ben's banana-peel-and-toothpick architectural design

USEFUL INFO

The back of every notebook has stuff that's supposed to be handy for school. Well, finally here's a REAL page of:

Table of Food Measure

All you need to know is which day is Pizza Day — ignore all other cafeteria offerings (or you'll be sorry!)

DON'T try the shepherd's pie — it might have a shepherd in it!

Ball Chart

The less round the ball, the less it will bounce.

DON'T pick a ball that looks like a whoopy cushion!

Table of Homework

(or Homework Table unless you do your homework on the floor)

one worksheet = ½ hour

one book report = stalling for an hour, then working for an hour

4a+2a=
6a-7a=
1.3 x 2.5=
6.8 x 7.1=

twenty math problems = misery all afternoon and time calculating that could have been spent watching TV

BBRRRNG! BBRRNG!

WAKE UP! TIME FOR SCHOOL!

Table of Time Measure

Monday – Ugh! Have to get up early again.

Tuesday – Groan! A whole week of school ahead.

Wednesday – Stuck right in the middle of the week.

Thursday – Hey, this is getting to be fun!

Friday – Yay! A great day AND the weekend ahead!

Saturday – PERFECT! A day all for me!

Sunday – Can't enjoy it knowing that tomorrow is ... MONDAY again!

Table of Linear Measure

The line you're in is always the longest and the slowest.

Worst lines: lining up for the bus, for field trips, for lunch
Best lines: lining up for fire drills

I've graduated from:

lunchboxes with characters on them

← Mr. Google-eyes

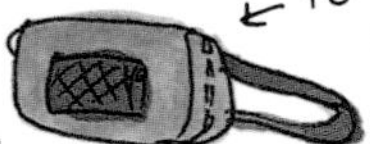

← to insulated high-tech containers in fashion colors

I used to have easy, fun homework →

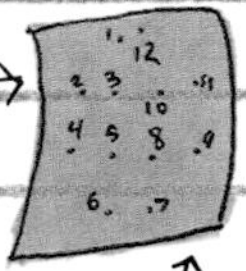

connect-the-dots

I've gone from thick markers, drawing like this

So! Now you're all set for school. You won't be swallowed by oral reports, poisoned by cafeteria food, or trampled by wild science projects. You may have close calls and near misses, but YOU WILL SURVIVE!

to cool gel pens, drawing like this

hands behind back to avoid drawing them

notice relaxed smile, not tense or worried at all!

prepared survivalist with backpack, hard hat, emergency supply kit, and, most important of all, brain packed with skills and tips to face *any* school horror

now I have tons of hard work

ADDED BONUS FUN STICKERS!
You can use these on your book covers, binders, pencil cases, homework — even on yourself. But don't eat, fold, spindle, or mutilate them. And forget about using them in your science project. For anything else, GO FOR IT!